LEVEL 1 READER

Fairy Hill

Luna and the Lost Shell

by Cari Meister
illustrated by Erika Meza

SCHOLASTIC INC.

For Benjamin—Forever Peter Pan

Library of Congress Cataloging-in-Publication Data
Names: Meister, Cari, author. | Meza, Erika, illustrator.
Title: Luna and the lost shell / by Cari Meister; illustrated by Erika Meza.
Description: New York, NY : Scholastic Inc., 2017. | Series: Fairy Hill [2]; | Summary: The fairy
ball is tonight, but someone has taken the magic shell which powers the glow globes, and
nobody wants to dance in the dark—Luna, Ruby and May find that chipmunk took it to light
his house, and Luna earns her big wings by making him a magic lamp in exchange for returning
the shell. Identifiers: LCCN 2016054942 | ISBN 9781338121827 (pbk.) Subjects: LCSH: Fairies—
Juvenile fiction. | Magic—Juvenile fiction. | CYAC: Fairies—Fiction. | Magic—Fiction. Classification:
LCC PZ7.M515916 Lr 2017 | DDC [E]—dc23 LC record available at https://lccn.loc.gov/2016054942

10 9 8 7 6 5 4 3 2 1   17 18 19 20 21

Printed in U.S.A.   40
First printing 2017

Book design by Steve Ponzo

The Fairy Ball is tonight.
There is so much to do!

May hangs shiny ribbons.
Her flyer, Dot, helps.

Luna and Star set up a music game.

Ruby and Ace make magic cupcakes.
Ruby tests the frosting.

Her wings turn bright blue.
Ruby uses her wand to fix them.

"Your big wings are so pretty," May tells Ruby.
"I wonder when the Fairy Queen will give me mine."

"We will earn ours by doing something brave, kind, or helpful," says Luna.

Then, the lights go out.

"Why did the glow globes go dark?" asks Ruby.

"Oh no! We cannot have a ball in the dark!"
says Luna.

Ring-a ling-ling! Ring-a ling-ling!

"The Fairy Queen is coming!" says Luna.

"Maybe someone is getting her big wings!"
says May.

But the Fairy Queen was not there to give out big wings.

"Fairy Hill's glow globes are powered by the magic shell. But the shell is missing! If we do not find it soon, I will have to cancel the ball," the Fairy Queen says.

"We must find the shell!" says May.
The friends look for clues.

"Look!" Luna says. "Chipmunk tracks!"

The girls follow the tracks.
They go past the big rock.

"The tracks stop here," says Ruby.

"The chipmunk must be nearby."

"Shhh," says Luna. "I hear something."

SCRITCH-SCRITCH

"I see the chipmunk!" says May.

"Does he have the magic shell?" asks Ruby.

"Something is glowing in his house," Luna says.

The fairies look in the window.
There is the shell!

"How can we get the shell back?" asks Ruby.

"I have an idea," says Luna.

"Let's make the chipmunk a special lamp.

Then he won't need our shell to light up his home."

The friends gather an acorn and fireflies.

Luna taps her wand.

The lamp glows.

"The chipmunk will love it!" says May.

The girls knock on the chipmunk's door.
"It looks like you are using our magic
shell to light your home," says Luna.
"But the fairies need it back," adds May.

"We made you a special lamp," Luna says.
"Can we trade?"
The chipmunk chatters.
He loves his new lamp!

"Your idea worked!" May tells Luna.
"Let's go!" says Ruby.
The fairies race to the castle.

They return the magic shell just in time.

The Fairy Ball begins.

Ring-a ling-ling! Ring-a ling-ling!

"The Fairy Queen!" says May.

"Luna," the Fairy Queen says.
"You were clever and kind. You brought back
the magic shell and saved the Fairy Ball.
Tonight you earn your big wings."

The Fairy Queen taps her magic wand.
Luna's wings grow.
They sparkle and shimmer.

"Your wings are pretty," says Ruby.
"They are so soft," says May.

Luna flaps her big wings.
"Let's dance!" she says.